The Jungle Book

Treasury of Illustrated Classics™

The Jungle Book

by
Rudyard Kipling

Adapted by
C. Louise March

Illustrated by
Julia Lundman

Modern Publishing
A Division of Unisystems, Inc.
New York, New York 10022

Series UPC: 39305

Cover art by Julia Lundman

Contents

=== ❦ ===

TIGER–TIGER

RIKKI-TIKKI-TAVI

TOOMAI OF THE ELEPHANTS

Mowgli's Brothers

CHAPTER 1

Mowgli Finds a Family

It was seven o'clock on a warm evening in the Seeonee hills when Father Wolf woke up. He gave himself a good scratch, yawned, and spread out his paws. Mother Wolf lay with her big gray nose across her four small, squealing cubs. The moon shone into the mouth of their cave.

"It is time to hunt again," Father Wolf said. He was going to spring out of the cave and start downhill when a little shadow with a bushy tail passed by.

"Good luck to you, Chief of the Wolves. Good luck and let your noble children have strong white teeth. May you never forget the hungry in this world."

It was Tabaqui, the jackal. The wolves of India hated Tabaqui because he was a mischief-maker. He was a tattletale and he ate from the village garbage. They feared him because he had fits and ran through the forest biting everything in his way. Even the brave tigers would run and hide when Tabaqui ran wild.

"There is no food here," Father Wolf said stiffly.

"For a wolf, no," Tabaqui said, "but for a poor one like me, a dry bone is a feast." He darted to the back of the cave, where he found the bone of a buck with some meat on it, and sat happily cracking the end and licking his lips.

"Thank you for this good meal," he said. "How beautiful are the noble children! How large are their eyes! The children of kings are men from the beginning."

Of course, Tabaqui knew very well that there was nothing so unlucky as

to compliment the children to their faces. It pleased him to see Mother Wolf's and Father Wolf's discomfort.

"Shere Khan has moved his hunting grounds," continued Tabaqui spitefully. "He will hunt among these hills for the next moon, so he has told me."

Shere Khan was the tiger that lived near the Waingunga River, twenty miles away.

"He has no right!" Father Wolf said angrily. "By the Law of the Jungle he

cannot change his quarters without warning. He will frighten every head of game within ten miles."

"His mother did not call him the Lame One for nothing," Mother Wolf said quietly. "Shere Khan has been lame in one foot from his birth. That is why he has only killed cattle. Now the villagers of the Waingunga are angry with him, and he has come here to anger our villagers. They will search the jungle for him, and we will have to run when they set the grass on fire."

"Shall I tell him of your gratitude?" Tabaqui asked sarcastically.

"Out!" Father Wolf snapped.

"I will go," Tabaqui said quietly. "You can hear Shere Khan for yourself, below. I should have saved myself the trouble of giving you the message."

CHAPTER 2

Shere Khan Hunts a Man-Cub

Father Wolf listened. Below in the valley that ran down to a little river he heard the dry, angry whine of a tiger that has caught nothing.

"The fool!" Father Wolf said. "To begin a night's work with that noise! Does he think that our buck are like his fat Waingunga bulls?"

"Hush. Tonight Shere Khan hunts neither bull nor buck," Mother Wolf said. "It is Man he is looking for."

"Man!" Father Wolf exclaimed, showing all of his white teeth. "Are there not enough beetles and frogs in the tanks that he must eat Man, and on our ground, too?"

The Law of the Jungle forbids every beast to eat Man, except when he is killing to show his children how to kill. Also, he must hunt outside the hunting grounds of his pack. This is because, when a man is killed, other men come to hunt the Jungle People and set the grass on fire to kill them.

The low purring noise had been rising from every corner of the jungle. Now it ended in the full-throated "Aaarh!" of the tiger's charge. Then there was an

anguished howl from Shere Khan.

"He has missed," Mother Wolf said.

Father Wolf ran out of the cave. Shere Khan was muttering savagely as he tumbled about in the scrub.

"The fool has jumped at a campfire and burned his feet," Father Wolf grunted. "Tabaqui is with him."

"Something is coming uphill," Mother Wolf cautioned. "Get ready."

The bushes rustled a little, and Father Wolf dropped down, ready to

leap. "Look!" he snapped. "A man-cub!"

Directly in front of him, holding on to a low branch, stood a naked boy. He was a soft, dimpled little creature. He looked up into Father Wolf's face and laughed.

"I have never seen a man-cub," Mother Wolf said. "Bring it here."

Father Wolf gently took hold of the child by his neck and brought him to Mother Wolf.

"He's so little—and bold!" Mother Wolf said softly. The boy was pushing his way between the cubs to get close to the warm hide. "He is taking his meal with the others!" she cried. "Now, was there ever a wolf that could boast of a man-cub among her children?"

"I have heard of such a thing, but never in our pack or in my time," Father Wolf said. "He is small and unprotected. But see, he looks up and is not afraid."

At that moment, Shere Khan thrust

his great square head and shoulders into the cave, blocking out the moonlight. Tabaqui, behind him, squeaked, "My lord, it went in here!"

"Shere Khan does us great honor," Father Wolf said, but his eyes were very angry. "What does Shere Khan need?"

"A man-cub went this way," he answered. "Its parents have run off. Give it to me."

Father Wolf knew that Shere Khan would not be able to enter the cave

because he was too big. Even where he was, Shere Khan's shoulders and forepaws were cramped.

"The Wolves are a free people," Father Wolf stated. "They take orders from the head of the pack and not from any striped cattle-killer. The man-cub is ours."

"Am I to stand nosing into your dog's den for what I am due? It is I, Shere Khan, who speaks!"

His roar filled the cave with thunder. Mother Wolf shook herself clear of her cubs and sprang forward. Her eyes were like two green moons in the darkness, facing the blazing eyes of Shere Khan.

"And it is I, the Demon, who answers. The man-cub is mine! He will live to run with the pack. He will hunt with the pack, and in the end he will hunt Shere Khan! Now go!" Mother Wolf roared.

So Shere Khan backed out of the cave mouth, growling. When he was clear, he shouted, "Each dog barks in his own yard! We will see what the pack says to this fostering of man-cubs. The cub is mine, you bush-tailed thieves!"

Mother Wolf threw herself down, panting among the cubs. Father Wolf said, "Shere Khan speaks this much truth. The cub must be shown to the pack. Will you still keep him, Mother?"

"Keep him!" she gasped. "He came naked by night, alone and very hungry. Yet he was not afraid! Look, he has pushed one of my cubs to one side already. Shere Khan would have killed him and run off to the Waingunga while the villagers here hunted through all of our lairs seeking revenge! I will keep him. Be still, little frog. I will call you Mowgli the Frog. The time will come when you will hunt Shere Khan as he has hunted you."

"But what will the pack say?" Father Wolf asked.

CHAPTER 3
A Meeting at the Council Rock

The Law says that any wolf may, when he marries, withdraw from the pack he belongs to. But as soon as his cubs are old enough to stand on their feet, he must bring them to the pack Council, which is held once a month at full moon so that the other wolves can identify them. After the inspection, the cubs are free to run where they please. A grown wolf of the pack cannot kill one of the cubs until the cub has killed its first buck. If a grown wolf does not obey this rule, the punishment is death.

Father Wolf waited until his cubs could run a little. Then, on the night of

the pack meeting, he took them, Mowgli, and Mother Wolf to the Council Rock—a hilltop covered with stones and boulders where a hundred wolves could meet unseen by others in the jungle.

Akela, also known as the Lone Wolf, was their leader. He was stretched out on his rock and, below him, forty or more wolves of different sizes, colors, and ages sat.

Akela knew the ways of men. Twice in his youth he had fallen into a wolf trap, and once he had been beaten and left for dead. From his rock, Akela would cry, "You know the Law. Look well!" The anxious mothers would repeat his call.

Finally the moment arrived for Mowgli to come before the pack. Mother Wolf's neck bristles rose as Father Wolf pushed Mowgli into the center, where he sat laughing and playing with some pebbles that glistened in the moonlight.

A roar rose up from behind the rocks. "The cub is mine. Give him to me," Shere Khan bellowed. "What have the Free People to do with a man-cub?"

Akela didn't even twitch his ears. "Look well, wolves! What have the Free People to do with orders from any but the Free People?" he replied.

Many in the pack joined in a chorus of growls. A young wolf flung back Shere Khan's question to Akela. "What have the Free People to do with a Man-cub?"

The Law of the Jungle says that if there is any dispute over the right of a

cub to be accepted by the pack, he must be spoken for by at least two members who are not the cub's parents.

"Who speaks for this cub?" Akela asked. No one answered.

Then someone came forward to speak for Mowgli. But it wasn't one of the wolves. It was old Baloo, the sleepy brown bear who taught the cubs the Law of the Jungle. Baloo was the only other creature that was allowed at the pack meeting. Baloo could move about

among the wolves as he liked because he ate only nuts and roots and honey.

"I speak for the man-cub," he said. "Let him run with the pack. I will teach him the Law."

"Baloo has spoken," Akela said. "Who speaks besides Baloo?"

A black shadow dropped down into the center of the circle. It was Bagheera, the black panther. Bagheera was as cunning as Tabaqui, as bold as the wild buffalo, and as reckless as the wounded elephant. His voice was as soft as wild honey dripping from a tree, and his skin softer than down.

"I have no right in your assembly," he purred, "but the Law says that if there is a doubt about a new cub that is not a killing matter, the life of that cub may be bought at a price. The Law does not say who may or may not pay that price. Am I right?"

"Listen to Bagheera," the young wolves said. "The cub can be bought for a price. It is the Law."

"It is a shame to kill a naked cub. Baloo has spoken on his behalf. Now I will add one fat bull, just killed, not half a mile from here, if you will accept the man-cub," Bagheera said.

"What harm can a naked frog do to us?" one wolf said.

"Let him run with the pack," said another. Others cried out, "Where is the bull, Bagheera?" and "Let him be accepted."

Mowgli's attention remained fixed on

the pebbles. He didn't notice when the wolves came over to look at him. At last they all went down the hill to find the dead bull, and only Akela, Bagheera, Baloo and Mowgli's protectors were left. Shere Khan roared. He was angry that Mowgli had not been handed over to him.

"Yes, Shere Khan," Bagheera said under his whiskers. "The time will come when this naked thing will make you roar to another tune, or I know nothing of man."

"Men and their cubs are very wise. He may be a help in time," Akela said to Father Wolf. "Train him as you would one of the Free People."

CHAPTER 4

Mowgli Learns the Law of the Jungle

Now we must skip ten or eleven years and only guess at the life that Mowgli led among the wolves, because if it were written out it would fill many books. He grew up with the cubs, but they were fully grown while he still was a child. Father Wolf taught him all about the Law of the Jungle so that Mowgli could recognize every sound and know about all of the other creatures and their ways.

When he wasn't busy with lessons, Mowgli sat out in the sun and slept, and ate and went to sleep again. When he felt dirty or hot he swam in the pools of the forest. When he wanted honey, he climbed up trees to get it. Bagheera showed him how to do it.

When he took his place at the pack meetings, Mowgli discovered that if he stared hard at a wolf, the wolf would be the first to drop its eyes to the ground. Mowgli made a game of this, delighting in this newly found source of power. But Mowgli was also becoming a friend to the wolves. Often he would pick long thorns out of the pads of their paws.

Sometimes at night, his curiosity led him down the hillside to the places inhabited by men. Bagheera had shown

him a trap—a square box with a drop gate—so cunningly hidden in the jungle that he nearly walked into it. Since then, Mowgli mistrusted his own kind.

More than anything, he loved to go with Bagheera into the dark heart of the forest. There they slept all day. Then, at night, Mowgli watched how Bagheera sought his prey. "All of the jungle is yours," Bagheera told him, "but for the sake of the bull that bought your life, you must never touch cattle, young or old. That is the Law of the Jungle." Mowgli faithfully obeyed.

Mother Wolf told him that Shere Khan could not be trusted, and that someday he must kill the tiger. A young wolf would never have forgotten her forceful instruction, but Mowgli was a young boy and soon forgot it.

Shere Khan was always crossing Mowgli's path. As Akela grew older, the crafty Shere Khan saw an opportunity to influence the younger wolves. They followed the lame tiger when he was looking for scraps and listened to his prattle. Shere Khan flattered the young wolves, and teased them about not being able to look Mowgli in the eye. The young wolves growled and bristled. Akela would never have permitted such a thing when he was in full command of his power.

Although Mowgli was not troubled by Shere Khan's threats, Bagheera knew everything that happened among the pack and warned his pupil. "Why should I be afraid?" Mowgli asked.

"Open your eyes, Little Brother. Shere Khan will not dare to kill you in the jungle. But remember, Akela is very old. Many of the wolves that have watched out for you are old, as well, and the young wolves have listened to Shere Khan's talk. Soon, you will be a man. Then there will be trouble."

"I was born in the jungle," Mowgli said. "I have obeyed the Law of the

Jungle, and there is no wolf of ours from whose paws I have not pulled a thorn. Surely they are my brothers!"

Bagheera sighed. "Little Brother," he said, "feel under my jaw." Mowgli felt under Bagheera's silky chin, where the giant rolling muscles were hidden by glossy hair. In a few moments, he came upon a little bald spot.

"No one in the jungle knows that I carry this mark—the mark of the man's collar," Bagheera said. "And yet, Little Brother, I was born among men, and it was among men that my mother died,

in the cages of the Maharaja's palace. This is the reason that I paid the price for you years ago at the pack meeting. You and I were both born among men. I had never seen the jungle. They fed me behind bars from an iron pan until one night I broke the lock with one blow of my paw and escaped. And because I learned the ways of men, I became more powerful in the jungle."

"Yes," Mowgli answered. "All in the jungle fear Bagheera—all except Mowgli."

"As I returned to the jungle, so you

must go live among men. If you don't, you will be killed. The wolves do not trust you. They lower their eyes when you stare at them."

Mowgli's dark eyebrows came together.

"Listen to me," Bagheera said. "When Akela misses a kill—and his strength ebbs with each day—the pack will turn against him. They will hold a Council meeting and then—" Bagheera paused. "I have it!" he suddenly cried out. "Go to the village and take some of the Red Flower that they grow. The Red Flower will protect you better than anyone in the jungle."

By Red Flower, Bagheera meant fire. Every beast lived in deadly fear of it.

"I will do as you say," Mowgli promised, "but are you sure that all of this is Shere Khan's doing?"

"I am sure, Little Brother."

"Then I will make sure that Shere Khan gets his due," Mowgli said, bounding away.

CHAPTER 5

The Red Flower

Mowgli ran swiftly through the wild forest. He stopped at his cave and looked down into the valley. Mother Wolf knew something was wrong and asked what troubled him.

"Some talk about Shere Khan," he answered. "I hunt among the plowed fields tonight," he added as he raced off. He stopped again at the stream at the bottom of the valley and heard the sounds of the pack hunting. The young wolves howled, "Akela! Let the Lone Wolf show his strength. Spring, Akela!"

Akela must have sprung and missed, for Mowgli heard the snap of Akela's teeth and then a yelp as the deer knocked him over. Mowgli didn't wait to hear more. He dashed toward the village.

He pressed his face close to the window of a hut and watched the fire on the hearth. He saw a woman get up and feed the fire during the night with black rocks. And when the morning came and the mists were all white and cold, he saw a man's child pick up a wicker pot plastered inside with earth, fill it with red-hot rocks, put it under his blanket, and go out to tend the cows.

"If a cub can do it, there is nothing to fear," Mowgli told himself. So Mowgli walked toward the boy, took the pot from his hand, and disappeared into the mist.

As he walked, Mowgli fed the fire as he had seen the woman do. Halfway up the hill he met Bagheera.

"Akela has missed," the panther reported. "They would have killed him last night, but they needed you, also. They looked for you on the hill."

"I am ready. See!" Mowgli said, holding up the fire-pot.

For the rest of the day, Mowgli sat in the cave and tended the fire, dipping dry branches in to find one that satisfied him.

In the evening, Tabaqui came to say, quite rudely, that Mowgli was now wanted at the Council Rock. Mowgli laughed until Tabaqui ran away. Then Mowgli went to the meeting.

Akela lay by the side of his rock, signaling that pack leadership was now

open. Shere Khan and his followers walked about menacingly. Bagheera lay close to Mowgli, and the fire-pot was between Mowgli's knees. When they were all gathered together, Shere Khan spoke—something he never would have done when Akela was in his prime.

Bagheera nudged Mowgli, who sprang to his feet and cried, "Free People, does Shere Khan lead the pack? What has a tiger to do with our leadership?"

"Silence, man-cub!" some yelled, while others shouted, "Let him speak. He has kept our Law." At last the seniors of the pack thundered, "Let the dead wolf speak." When a leader of the pack has missed his kill, he is called the dead wolf as long as he lives, which is not long.

"For twelve seasons I have led you," began Akela. "Not one of you has been trapped or injured. Now I have missed my kill. You all know that you brought me to an untried buck to reveal my weakness. It was cleverly done. And now, by our Law, you have the right to kill me. I ask, who comes to make an end of Akela? For, by our Law, it is my right that you come one by one."

No one answered, since no wolf cared to fight Akela alone to the death. But Shere Khan roared, "Forget this fool. He is doomed to die. It is the man-cub that I want. He was mine from the start. Give him to me."

Wolves' voices rang up on all sides, all saying that Mowgli should return to his own kind.

"And turn all of the people and hunters of the villages against us?" Shere Khan sneered. "No, give him to me. He is a man, and none of us can look him in the eyes."

Akela lifted his head again and said, "He has eaten our food. He has slept with us. He has driven game for us. He has followed our Law."

Bagheera reminded everyone that he

paid for Mowgli's life with a bull. "The worth of a bull is little, but Bagheera's honor is something that he will, perhaps, fight for," Bagheera said very gently.

"No man-cub can run with the people of the jungle," Shere Khan bellowed. "Give him to me!"

Akela broke in, "I know I must die, or I would offer my life for his. He is our brother, raised among us. His enemies are cowards, taught by Shere Khan to go against our Law, eating cattle and

snatching children from the village. The honor of our pack is at stake. If you let this man-cub go back to his people, I will die without a fight and save the pack at least three lives."

When most of the wolves began to gather around Shere Khan, Akela knew he had lost.

"Now the business is in your hands," Bagheera said to Mowgli. "We must fight."

Mowgli stood up, the fire-pot in his hands. He was furious and sad that the

wolves had never revealed how they felt about him.

"I have heard you say I am a man," Mowgli said. "I would have lived as a wolf in the pack to my life's end, but now I understand that this is not to be. I can no longer call you my brothers. The matter is now in my hands, for I am a man, as you say, and I have brought the Red Flower!"

With that, Mowgli flung the fire-pot on the ground. Some of the red coals lit a tuft of dried moss. When it caught fire and flared up, the wolves drew back in terror before the leaping flames. Mowgli thrust his dead branch into the fire until the twigs lit and crackled. Then he whirled it before the cowering wolves.

"You now are the master," Bagheera murmured to him. "Save Akela. He is your friend."

Mowgli nodded. "I will leave you alone," he said to the wolves, "but I will be more merciful than you have been.

Because I was all but your brother in blood, I promise that when I am a man among men I will not betray you as you have betrayed me."

He kicked the fire with his foot, and the sparks flew up. "There will be no war between any in the pack, but there is a debt to pay before I go." He strode toward Shere Khan and caught him by the tuft on his chin. Bagheera followed. "Up, dog!" Mowgli cried. "Get up, when a man speaks, or you will feel the heat from this blaze!"

Shere Khan's ears lay flat back on his head, and he shut his eyes, for the blazing branch was very near. Mowgli hit Shere Khan over the head with the branch, and the tiger whimpered in fear.

"Quiet, jungle cat. Go now. But remember that the next time I come to the Council Rock, it will be with your hide on my head." To the others, he said, "Akela goes free to live as he pleases. You will not kill him. Go now,

all of you!"

The fire was burning furiously at the end of the branch, and Mowgli struck out with it around the circle. The howling wolves ran off, with the sparks burning their fur.

At last only Akela, Bagheera, and some wolves that had spoken up for Mowgli remained. Now that it was quiet again, Mowgli noticed a pain inside him. It hurt as nothing had hurt him before. He sobbed.

"What is it? Am I dying, Bagheera?" he asked.

"No, Little Brother. Those are tears. They will not harm you," Bagheera said. "Now you are a man. The jungle is closed to you. Let the tears fall."

So Mowgli sat and cried until he was exhausted. When he was finished, he said, "Now I am ready to go to the village. But first I must say farewell to Mother Wolf."

"You will not forget me?" Mowgli asked her when he reached the cave.

"Come to the foot of the hill and we will talk to you, and we will come into the croplands to play with you by night," the cubs broke in.

"Yes, come soon!" Father Wolf and Mother Wolf said together. "Oh, wise Little Frog, come again soon."

Mowgli nodded. The dawn was beginning to break when he finally went down the hillside alone.

Kaa's
Hunting

CHAPTER 1
Mowgli Learns the Master Words

Whatis told here happened some time before Mowgli left the pack and paid back Shere Khan for his treachery. It took place while Mowgli was learning the Law of the Jungle from Baloo.

Baloo was pleased to have Mowgli as a pupil. The boy learned his lessons quickly, unlike the young wolves.

As a man-cub, Mowgli needed to learn more than the Law. He was lucky to have both Baloo and Bagheera to guide him. Often Bagheera would come to see how his pet was getting on, and would purr with his head against a tree while Mowgli recited the day's lesson to Baloo.

Baloo taught him how to tell a rotten branch from a sturdy one, and how to speak politely to the wild bees when he found a hive. He taught him what to say to Mang the Bat when Mowgli disturbed him in the branches at noon.

Mowgli also learned the Strangers' Hunting Call. If the Jungle People hunted beyond their own grounds, the call must be repeated aloud until it is answered. It means, "Please allow me to hunt here because I am hungry." The answer is, "Hunt, then, for food, but not for pleasure."

Bagheera would have spoiled Mowgli, but Baloo did not allow it. Baloo would say, "Better he should be bruised from head to foot by me who loves him than that he should come to harm through ignorance."

Wise Baloo was teaching Mowgli the Master Words of the Jungle that would protect him from all the beasts. "I will call Mowgli and he will say them for you,"

Baloo told Bagheera. "Come, Little Brother!"

Mowgli slid down a tree trunk. He was very angry because of the work he had to do that day. "I come for Bagheera and not for you, old Baloo!" he said.

"That is no matter to me," Baloo said, but he was hurt by Mowgli's words. "Tell Bagheera the Master Words of the Jungle what you have learned."

"For which people?" Mowgli asked. "The jungle has many tongues. I know

them all." He was delighted to show off.

"See, Bagheera. Not one wolf cub has ever come back to thank his teacher," Baloo said. To Mowgli, he said, "Say the word for the Hunting People, if you can remember it."

"We be of one blood, you and I," Mowgli said, saying the words in the Bear accent used by all of the Hunting People.

Despite Mowgli's ingratitude, Baloo was happy to have such a fine pupil.

Mowgli was now well guarded because neither snake, bird, nor beast would hurt him.

"He fears no one," Baloo said, patting his big furry stomach with pride.

"Except his own tribe," Bagheera said under his breath. To Mowgli, he said, "Be careful of my ribs, Little Brother! What is all this dancing up and down?"

Mowgli had been trying to get Bagheera's attention by pulling at the

panther's shoulder fur and kicking hard. He was now shouting at the top of his voice, "I will have a tribe of my own and lead them through the branches all day."

"What is this new folly, my little dreamer?" Bagheera asked.

"Yes, and throw branches and dirt at old Baloo," Mowgli went on. "They have promised me this."

Baloo's big paw scooped Mowgli off Bagheera's back. The boy could see that Baloo was angry.

"Mowgli," Baloo said, "you have been talking with the Monkey People."

Mowgli looked to see if Bagheera was angry, too. The panther's eyes were as hard as stones.

"The Monkey People are without a law. They will eat anything," Bagheera said.

"When Baloo hurt my head, I went away, and the gray apes came down from the trees and had pity on me. No one else cared," Mowgli said.

"Their pity will do you no good!" Baloo snorted. "And then, man-cub?"

"And then they gave me nuts and pleasant things to eat, and they carried me in their arms up to the top of the trees. They said I was their blood brother and should be their leader someday."

"They have no leader," said Bagheera. "They lie. They have always lied."

"Why didn't you tell me about the Monkey People, Baloo? They stand on their feet as I do. They do not hit me with their hard paws. They play all day.

Bad Baloo!" Mowgli cried.

"I've taught you the laws of all of the beasts that have laws. The Monkey People do not have any law. They are outcasts. We of the jungle have no dealings with them."

He had hardly spoken when a shower of nuts and twigs spattered down through the branches. They heard rough noises coming from above as the angry apes jumped up and down among the thin tree branches.

"Little Frog, remember this. Stay away from them," Baloo warned sternly.

CHAPTER 2

Kidnapped by the Monkey People

Since the Monkey People lived in the trees, they rarely got in the way of the Jungle People. But whenever they found a sick wolf or wounded beast, the monkeys tormented it. They stirred up a lot of trouble and contributed nothing to the life of the jungle.

Since the other beasts of the jungle ignored them, the Monkey People were thrilled to have captured Mowgli's attention. One of them said that Mowgli would be useful in their tribe. So they quietly followed Baloo, Bagheera, and their pupil through the jungle. Then, when it was time for the midday nap, they saw their chance. Meanwhile,

Mowgli, who was very ashamed, slept peacefully between his protectors, having resolved to stay away from the Monkey People.

The next thing Mowgli knew, he felt the press of strong hands on his legs and arms and branches fluttering over his face. Looking down through the boughs of a tree, he saw Baloo rise and cry out as Bagheera bounded up the tree trunk with his teeth showing.

The monkeys howled in triumph as they scattered to higher branches, out of Bagheera's reach. Two of the strongest monkeys caught Mowgli under the arms and swung him through the treetops, twenty feet at a bound. The motion made Mowgli sick, but he couldn't help but feel a thrill at the wild rush and cries of victory. From the tops of the trees, Mowgli could see clear across the jungle for miles.

Mowgli knew that he had to send word back to Baloo and Bagheera, who by this point were far behind. When he

looked down, Mowgli could only see the top sides of the branches, so he stared upward and saw, far away, Chil the Kite. Chil was balancing and wheeling as he kept watch over the jungle. He had seen that the monkeys were carrying something, and dropped a few hundred yards to find out whether their load was good to eat. When he realized that it was a man-cub and heard him give the Kite Call, Chil was quite surprised.

"Mark my trail!" Mowgli shouted. "Tell Baloo of the Seeonee Pack and Bagheera of the Council Rock."

"In whose name?" Chil asked. He had never seen Mowgli before, but of course he had heard of him.

"Mowgli the Frog," Mowgli shouted.

Chil nodded and rose up until he was no bigger than a speck of dust, and there he hung, watching with his telescope eyes.

"They never go far," Chil said with a

chuckle. "And this time they are in for trouble, if I know Baloo and Bagheera." So Chil gathered his feet up under him and waited.

While Mowgli was being spirited away by the monkeys, Baloo and Bagheera argued with each other. Bagheera had tried to climb up to Mowgli, but the thin branches broke beneath his weight and he slipped down, his claws full of bark.

"Why didn't you warn the man-cub?" he roared to poor Baloo, who was lum-

bering off in the hope of overtaking the monkeys. "A lot of good all of those lessons will do now."

"Hush. We may catch them yet," Baloo panted.

"At that speed!" Bagheera laughed. "Sit still and think! This is no time for chasing. They may drop him if we follow too close."

"The Monkey People are crazy," Bagheera continued, "but Mowgli is wise and well taught. Above all, he has eyes that make the Jungle People afraid. But the Monkey People are evil and are not afraid of us, because they are out of our reach." Bagheera licked one forepaw thoughtfully.

Suddenly Baloo smacked his head and shouted, "I am a fool! Why didn't I think of this before? The Monkey People fear Kaa the Rock Snake. He can climb as well as they can. He steals the young monkeys in the night."

Bagheera doubted that Kaa would

help them. But Baloo said, "He is very old and very cunning. And he is always hungry. Promise him many goats."

"Kaa sleeps for a month after he has eaten. He may be sleeping now. And if he is awake, he will want to kill his own goats," Bagheera said.

Baloo would not be swayed by Bagheera's doubts. "You and I together will make him see that Mowgli must be rescued," he said. Then they left together to find Kaa.

CHAPTER 3
Kaa Helps Out

They found Kaa basking in the afternoon sun. Kaa put on quite a show for his visitors. He looked splendid as he darted his head along the ground and twisted his body—which measured thirty feet—into knots and curves.

"Look at him lick his lips," Baloo said. "He hasn't eaten. Be careful, Bagheera! He is always a little blind after he has changed his skin, and quick to strike."

Kaa's threat was not poison. Kaa's weapon was his strength. When he wrapped his huge coils around an enemy, there was no more to be said.

"Good hunting!" Baloo cried, sitting up on his haunches.

"Good hunting for us all," Kaa answered. "One of us at least needs food. Is there any news of game afoot? A doe, perhaps, or even a young buck?"

"We're hunting," Baloo said casually, trying not to make Kaa suspicious.

"Allow me to come with you," Kaa said. "The branches are not what they were when I was young. Now they are all rotten twigs and dry boughs."

"Maybe your weight has something to do with it," Baloo suggested.

"Perhaps," Kaa replied. "But I think the fault is this new timber. I almost fell on my last hunt. The noise of my slipping woke the Monkey People, and they taunted me with evil names."

"You footless, yellow earthworm," Bagheera said under his whiskers.

"Sssss!" Kaa hissed. "Have they ever called me that?"

"Something like that. They have no shame and will say anything—even that you have lost all your teeth and will not

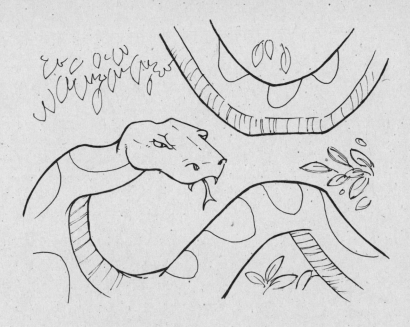

face anything bigger than a kid because you are afraid of the he-goat's horns," Bagheera said sweetly.

Now a snake, especially a wary old python like Kaa, rarely shows that he is angry. But Baloo and Bagheera could see the big muscles bulge on either side of Kaa's throat.

"The Monkey People have moved their grounds," he said quietly. "Today I heard them whooping among the treetops."

"We're following them," Baloo said.

Kaa was curious. "It must be no small thing that sends you on the trail of the Monkey People," he said.

"Indeed," Baloo began. "I am no more than the old and sometimes foolish teacher of the Law to the Seeonee wolf-cubs, and Bagheera here—"

"Is Bagheera," the panther said, snapping his jaws shut, for he didn't believe in being humble. "Those nut-stealers and pickers of palm leaves have stolen our man-cub. Have you heard of Mowgli?"

"Ikki the Porcupine spoke of a man-

cub entering a wolf pack," Kaa replied. "But I did not believe it."

"It is true," Baloo said. "This man-cub is wise and bold. Besides, we love him."

"Right now, this man-cub is in the hands of the Monkey People, and we need your help," Bagheera interrupted. "You are the only one they fear."

"They have good reason to fear me," Kaa said. "They are foolish and vain. They drop whatever is entertaining them at the moment for anything new that happens to come along."

Baloo and Bagheera nodded.

"What else did they call me? Yellow fish, was it not?"

"Earthworm," Bagheera said. "The names are so shameful."

"Now, where did they go with the cub?" Kaa asked.

"Toward the sunset, I believe," Baloo said, shrugging his big shoulders. "We thought you would know, Kaa."

"How would I know?" Kaa asked. "I

do not hunt monkeys."

"Look up, Baloo of the Seeonee Wolf Pack!" a voice rang out.

Baloo looked up to see where the voice came from. It was Chil the Kite swooping down with the sun shining on his outspread wings. It was near Chil's bedtime, but he had been all over the jungle looking for Baloo.

"What is it?" Baloo asked.

"I have seen Mowgli with the Monkey People," Chil reported. "They have taken him beyond the river to the Monkey City. I have told the bats to watch through the night. Good hunting to all of you below!"

CHAPTER 4
The Cold Lairs

They all knew where the Monkey City was, but few of the Jungle People ever went there. An old deserted city, lost and buried in the jungle, this place was also known as the Cold Lairs.

"It is half a night's journey at full speed," Bagheera said.

Baloo looked worried, so he added, "I will go as fast as I can."

"We dare not wait for you, Baloo. You can follow along behind."

So Bagheera and Kaa raced ahead.

Soon Mowgli arrived with his captors at the Cold Lairs. The place was a heap of ruins. At first Mowgli was enchanted because he had never seen a city before. A king had built it long ago on a little hill. Trees had grown into and out of the walls, and wild creepers hung out of the windows of the towers. The crumbled remains of a palace crowned the hill. The rest of the city consisted of courtyards, fountains, and rows of roofless houses—all in the last stages of decay. The Monkey People thought this was far superior to the jungle. But Mowgli knew better.

The monkeys dragged Mowgli into one of their dwellings. For a while they played and danced around, but then they lost interest in him.

"I wish to eat," Mowgli said.

A number of the monkeys raced off to find nuts, but they began fighting on the road and didn't come back. Mowgli was angry as well as sore and hungry from his terrifying trip. So he left the lair to wander about the city, giving the Strangers' Hunting Call as he went. No one answered.

When he reached the city wall, some monkeys drew him back. They took him to a terrace above the reservoirs. The ruins of a white marble summerhouse stood in the center of the terrace. The domed roof had fallen halfway in and blocked an underground passage from the palace. But the marble fretwork on the walls—inlaid with precious stones of every color—was quite beautiful. The moon came up behind the hill and sent beams of light through the open work that cast shadows on the ground.

Mowgli wanted to sleep. He was tired of the monkeys' chattering. When a cloud came by and covered the moon, Mowgli said to himself, "If it were a big enough cloud, I might try to run away in the darkness. But I am too tired."

CHAPTER 5

Bagheera and Kaa
to the Rescue

Bagheera and Kaa were watching that same cloud. They had finally arrived at the Monkey City. They sat in a ditch and discussed how they might ambush the monkeys, for they were far outnumbered.

"I will go to the west wall," Kaa whispered, "and come down swiftly with the slope of the ground in my favor."

"I wish that Baloo were here, but we must do what we can," Bagheera said. "When that cloud covers the moon, I will go to the terrace. They are holding some sort of Council there."

Meanwhile, Mowgli still sat wondering what to do. Then he heard Bagheera's

light feet on the terrace and saw the
panther striking out in all directions at
the monkeys, who sat in a circle around
Mowgli, fifty or sixty deep.

Seeing that there was only one oppo-
nent, the monkeys closed over Bagheera,
biting, scratching and tearing at him. A
few others grabbed Mowgli, dragged him
up the wall of the summerhouse, and
pushed him through the hole of the broken dome. Mowgli fell as Baloo had
taught him, landing on his feet.

Mowgli quickly gave the Snake's Call. Soon he heard rustling and hissing all around him. He gave the call a second time. "Stand still, Little Brother, for thy feet may do us harm," the snake said.

Mowgli stood as quietly as he could, listening to the scuffling around him. Bagheera was putting up a good fight, but he was fighting for his life.

"Get to the water tanks, Bagheera!" Mowgli shouted.

When he heard Mowgli's voice, Bagheera felt a surge of courage. He worked his way to the reservoirs. As he arrived, he heard Baloo's war cry come trumpeting out of the jungle.

Baloo panted up to the terrace and disappeared as a wave of monkeys surrounded him. He stretched out his arms and grabbed a number of them in a huge bear hug. Then he began to bat them all away.

Mowgli heard a splash and knew that Bagheera had reached the tanks.

The monkeys could not follow him and they were enraged. Bagheera lifted his head from the water, gasped for breath, and then, in despair, gave the Snake's Call. Baloo, who certainly had enough to handle on his own, couldn't help chuckling at the prideful panther asking for help.

Kaa delivered his first stroke, hissing into the crowd around Baloo. The monkeys scattered, screaming, "Run! It is Kaa!" They had heard the stories told by

their elders about Kaa slithering through the night, stealing the strongest monkeys. Soon the monkeys were cowering in their hiding places, and all was silent.

Baloo sighed in relief. Mowgli heard Bagheera shaking his wet sides as he came up from the tank. Then the loud clamor broke out again. The monkeys leaped higher up the walls. They clung around the necks of the big stone idols and shrieked as they skipped along the battlements. Still captive in the summerhouse, Mowgli glared out at the monkeys.

"Get Mowgli out of that trap," Bagheera gasped.

"Kaa, we owe our lives to you," Baloo said. He had been mauled in the struggle and was a bit shaky.

Kaa shrugged off Baloo's thanks. "Where is the man-cub?" he asked.

"Here," Mowgli cried from the summerhouse. "I cannot climb out." The curve of

the broken dome was above his head.

Kaa found a crack in the marble tracery. He tapped it lightly with his head a few times and then, lifting six feet of his body off the ground, he sent off a round of smashing blows, leading with his nose. The wall broke and fell in a cloud of dust.

Freed from his prison, Mowgli leaped through the opening and ran to Baloo and Bagheera, flinging an arm around each of their necks.

Baloo hugged Mowgli and asked if he was hurt.

"I am sore, hungry, and bruised. But look at you—all of you have been hurt badly," Mowgli replied.

"And so have the Monkey People," Bagheera said, looking around at the dead monkeys on the terrace.

"Kaa saved us," Bagheera added.

Mowgli turned and saw the great Python's head swaying a foot above.

"So this is the man-cub," Kaa said.

"His skin is very soft."

Mowgli looked at Kaa and repeated the Snake's Call. "We are of one blood. Tonight I take my life from you. My kill shall be your kill if ever you are hungry."

Kaa's eyes twinkled. "Thank you, Little Brother," he said.

"I owe a debt to you and Baloo and Bagheera. Good hunting to you all, my masters," Mowgli replied.

Baloo nodded his approval. "Well said," he growled.

"He has a brave heart and a courteous tongue," Kaa said. "These will carry him far in the jungle. Now it is time to leave, and quickly. The moon sets, and soon there will not be enough light to see by." His gaze shifted to the monkeys huddled together on the walls and battlements.

Bagheera was still angry with Mowgli for causing so much trouble. "What says the Law of the Jungle, Baloo?" he asked.

Baloo was inclined to let Mowgli off easily, but he could not argue with the

Law, which says that remorse does not eliminate the need for punishment. He reminded Bagheera that Mowgli was very little.

"But he has done mischief," Bagheera said. "Mowgli, what do you have to say for yourself?"

"Nothing. I did wrong," Mowgli answered.

Bagheera gave Mowgli half a dozen love-taps. They would hardly have awakened one of his own cubs, but for a boy, they were pretty harsh. When it was all over, Mowgli bravely picked himself up without a word.

"Now," Bagheera said, "jump on my back, Little Brother, and we will go home."

Mowgli laid his head down on Bagheera's back and slept peacefully all the way.

Tiger-Tiger

CHAPTER 1
Mowgli
Finds a New Family

After Mowgli was forced to leave the pack, he went to the nearest village of men, but he decided not to stop there because it was too close to the jungle. Instead, he stayed on the road that went into the valley until he came to unfamiliar country. The valley opened into a great plain. A village was at one end of the plain; at the other end, the jungle gave way to grazing land, where cattle and buffalo were plenty.

A few young boys were tending the herds. When they saw Mowgli, they shouted and ran away. Mowgli kept walking, hoping to find some food. But when he came to the village, he found that the gate was closed.

Mowgli was not surprised, because he knew that men were afraid of the Jungle People. So he sat down to wait. When a man came out, Mowgli stood up, opened his mouth, and pointed inside to show that he wanted food. The man stared and ran back up the one street of the village, shouting for the priest. A large man dressed in white came to the gate. At least one hundred people, staring and shouting, were with him.

"Men folk have no better manners than the gray apes," Mowgli whispered as he frowned at the crowd.

"Look at the marks on his arms and legs. They are wolf bites. He is a wolf-child run away from the jungle," the priest stated.

Some of the women sighed in sympathy. "Poor child," one said. "Messua, he looks like your boy, who was taken by the tiger."

A woman with heavy copper rings on

her wrists and ankles peered at Mowgli. "He is thinner," she said, "but he has the look of my boy."

The crowd parted as Messua walked Mowgli to her hut. Messua was married to the wealthiest man in the village. Their home contained a red lacquered bedstead, a great earthen grain chest with raised patterns on it, and some copper cooking pots. A real looking-glass hung on the wall.

As Messua fed him with milk and

bread, she wondered whether Mowgli really was her son. "Nathoo," she said, using his given name. Mowgli did not recognize the name.

She decided that since it appeared that Mowgli didn't have any protectors, she would raise him like her own son. Although Mowgli felt uncomfortable, never having been under a roof, he relaxed when he saw that the windows were not barred. He could get away if he wanted to.

From Baloo, Mowgli learned the

importance of speaking the other beasts' languages. So as soon as Messua said a word, he imitated it almost perfectly. Before dark he had learned the names of many things in the hut.

When it was time to go to sleep, Mowgli went outside. He stretched out in the long grass at the edge of the field, but before he had closed his eyes a soft gray nose poked him under the chin.

It was Gray Brother, the firstborn of Mother Wolf's cubs. "Wake, Little Brother. I bring news," he said.

"Is everything well in the jungle?" Mowgli asked, hugging him.

"All but the wolves that were burned with the Red Flower," Gray Brother replied. "Shere Khan has gone far away until his coat grows back—he was badly singed from the fire. But he says that when he comes back, he plans to get even with you."

Mowgli smiled and said, "I also have made a little promise."

"You won't forget that you are a wolf, will you?" Gray Brother asked anxiously.

"Never," Mowgli reassured him. "I will always love my wolf family, but I can't forget that I was cast out of the pack."

"Men are only men, Little Brother. Their ways are not our ways. When I come down here again, I will wait for you in the bamboos at the edge of the grazing ground."

CHAPTER 2

Learning the Ways of Men

Just as Mowgli learned the Law of the Jungle, he had to learn the ways of men. This kept him very busy. Some things caused him great annoyance: wearing a cloth around his body, using money, and plowing to grow food. He couldn't see the use of these customs.

The little children in the village made fun of him because he didn't know their games and couldn't say their words correctly. This made Mowgli very angry, but the Law says that life in the jungle depends on keeping one's temper and leaving the small and defenseless alone.

Everyone was shocked at Mowgli's

strength, which by comparison with that of the beasts of the jungle was nothing. Mowgli used his strength to help the villagers but, because he did not understand the notion of class, he caused a good deal of trouble.

The priest scolded him for helping a lowly potter, whose donkey had slipped into a clay pit. The priest told Messua's husband to put Mowgli to work as punishment. But Mowgli was delighted when the village headman said he had to herd buffalo.

That night, Mowgli discovered other advantages of being appointed a village servant. He had to attend a meeting of the village club, which took place every evening on a platform under a fig tree. The men told wonderful tales, and Mowgli got to hear all of the village gossip.

Buldeo, the hunter, spoke about the jungle beasts until the eyes of the children, sitting outside the circle, glowed in wonder. Mowgli had to cover his face to

show that he was not laughing while Buldeo, his musket across his knees, moved from one fantastic story to another.

Buldeo said the tiger that had carried away Messua's son was a ghost-tiger. His body was inhabited by the ghost of an old, dishonest money-lender who had died some years ago. "This is true," he said, "because Purun Dass always limped from the blow that he got in a riot. The tiger that I speak of limps, too."

"That tiger limps because he was

born lame, as everyone knows," Mowgli interrupted.

Buldeo was speechless for a moment. Then he said, "If you are so wise, jungle brat, bring the hide to the government and collect the money put up for the tiger's life. If you know what is good for you, you won't talk when your elders are speaking."

"Very little of what Buldeo has told you of the jungle is true," Mowgli said as he rose to go.

Buldeo glared at Mowgli, and the headman said that it was time for the boy to go back to herding.

The village custom was for a few boys to take the cattle and buffalo out to graze early in the morning, then bring them back at night. So at dawn, Mowgli went through the village street sitting on the back of Rama, the great herd bull. The other buffalo followed. Mowgli made it very clear to the boys with him that he was master.

Mowgli drove the herd to the edge of the plain, where the Waingunga River comes out of the jungle. Then he climbed down from Rama's back and walked to the bamboos at the edge of the grazing ground.

Just as Gray Brother had promised, he was waiting there for Mowgli. Gray Brother asked why Mowgli was herding the cattle.

"I've been made a village herder, at least for a while," Mowgli said. "Do you have news of Shere Khan?"

"Shere Khan came back and waited for you. Game is scarce now, so he went off again. He said he would be back, and he means to kill you."

"For as long as he is gone, come or send one of the brothers to sit on that rock so I can see you when I come out of the village. When Shere Khan returns, wait for me in the ravine, by the tree in the center of the plain," Mowgli instructed.

CHAPTER 3
Shere Khan Returns

At last the day came when Gray Brother was not in the usual place. Mowgli directed the buffalo toward the ravine. Gray Brother sat by the tree, which was covered with golden flowers. The bristles on his back were raised.

"Last night Shere Khan crossed the plains with Tabaqui following your trail," Gray Brother reported.

"I am not afraid of Shere Khan, but Tabaqui is very cunning," Mowgli said, frowning.

"Don't worry," Gray Brother said. "I met Tabaqui at dawn. He said that Shere Khan plans to wait for you at the village gate this evening."

"Has he eaten, or does he hunt on an empty stomach?" Mowgli asked. The answer meant life or death to him.

"He killed a pig at dawn," Gray Brother answered. "Shere Khan could never fast, even for the sake of revenge."

"Shere Khan is a fool!" Mowgli said in disgust. "Where is he now?"

"He swam far down the Waingunga," Gray Brother replied.

Mowgli stood with his finger in his mouth, thinking. "The big ravine of the

Waingunga River opens out on the plain not half a mile from here. I can take the herd around through the jungle to the head of the ravine and then sweep down. But he would slink out at the foot. We must block that end. Can you cut the herd in two for me?" Mowgli asked.

"With pleasure," Gray Brother said, smiling. He turned away and dropped into a hole nearby. After a moment, a huge gray head popped up out of the hole.

It was Akela! Mowgli clapped his hands. "We have a big job to do, Akela. Cut the herd in two. Keep the cows and calves together, and the bulls and buffalo by themselves."

Mowgli climbed onto Rama's back. "Akela," he called, "drive the bulls to the left. Gray Brother, wait until we are gone. Then keep the cows together. Drive them to the foot of the ravine."

"How far?" Gray Brother asked.

"Until the sides are higher than Shere

Khan can jump," Mowgli shouted. "Keep them there until we come down."

Mowgli cheered them on as they worked. The other herd children, watching with the cattle half a mile away, hurried to the village as fast as their legs could carry them, crying that the buffalo had gone mad and run away.

Mowgli's plan was simple: He wanted to make a big circle uphill and get to the head of the ravine, then take the bulls down it and catch Shere Khan between the bulls and the cows. He knew that after a meal Shere Khan would not be in any condition to fight or climb up the sides of the ravine.

At last Mowgli rounded up the herd on a grassy patch that sloped steeply down to the ravine. From that height he could see across the treetops to the plain below. Mowgli saw with a great deal of satisfaction that the sides of the ravine ran nearly straight up and down, while the vines and creepers that hung over them would give no foothold to a tiger who wanted to get out.

"I must tell Shere Khan who comes. We have him in the trap," Mowgli said, putting his hands to his mouth and shouting down the ravine. The echoes bounced off of the rocks.

After a long pause, they heard a sleepy snarl.

"Who calls?" Shere Khan asked, and a splendid peacock fluttered up from the ravine, screeching.

"It is Mowgli, you cattle thief," Mowgli said triumphantly. "Hurry them down, Akela! Down, Rama!"

The herd pitched over, one after the other, the sand and stones spurting up around them. Once the stampede began, nothing could stop it. Before they were fairly in the bed of the ravine, Rama winded Shere Khan and bellowed.

Shere Khan heard the thunder of their hoofs, picked himself up, and hobbled down the ravine. There was no

way to escape, and he was willing to do anything but fight.

The bellowing herd splashed through the pool he had just left. Mowgli heard an answering bellow from the cows at foot of the ravine. Shere Khan turned, knowing that it was better to meet the bulls than the mother cows with their calves.

Then Rama tripped and trampled over something soft. With the bulls at his heels, he crashed into the other herd. The weaker buffalo were lifted off their feet by the shock of the impact. That charge carried both herds out into the plain, goring and stamping and snorting. Mowgli slipped off Rama's neck, laying about him right and left with his stick.

"Quick, Akela! Scatter them, or they will fight one another."

Akela and Gray Brother ran about nipping the beasts' legs. The herd turned to charge up the ravine again, but Mowgli managed to redirect Rama, and the others followed him.

Shere Khan hand been trampled on. He was dead.

"Brothers, Shere Khan died a dog's death," Mowgli said. He felt for the knife he carried in a sheath around his neck now that he lived with men. "His hide will look well on the Council Rock. We must get to work swiftly."

CHAPTER 4

Cast Out Once More

Aboy raised by men could not have skinned a ten-foot tiger alone, but Mowgli knew how the skin was fitted on and how to take it off. Mowgli slashed and tore at the skin for an hour while the wolves watched until he called on them to help tug or tear.

When he was well into his work, he felt a hand on his shoulder. Mowgli turned and saw Buldeo with his musket. The herd children had told the villagers about the stampede. Buldeo was angry that Mowgli hadn't taken better care of the herd.

When Buldeo had realized the situation, he was astounded. "It is the Lame

Tiger—and there is a large reward for his hide!" he said. "We will overlook your carelessness, and perhaps I will give you a tiny bit of the reward."

Mowgli disagreed with this plan, and let Buldeo know it. "I need the skin for my own use, old man," he said.

"You cannot talk that way to the chief hunter of the village," Buldeo spluttered. "I will not give you any money—only a big beating!"

Mowgli shook his head and called

Akela, who was hiding with Gray Brother.

The next thing Buldeo knew, he was stretched out on the grass with a huge gray wolf standing over him. Mowgli went on skinning.

Buldeo lay still. He was spooked by this boy who could skin a tiger and give orders to a wolf.

"You must be a great king," he choked out.

"Yes," Mowgli said, chuckling a little. "Let him go, Akela."

When Buldeo got to the village, he told a story of sorcery that made the priest look very grave.

Mowgli went on with his work. It was nearly twilight when he and the wolves had drawn the skin clear off Shere Khan's body.

"We must hide this and take the buffalo home! Help me, Akela," Mowgli said.

After they rounded up the herd, they traveled on to the village. Mowgli saw

lights and heard the temple bells ringing. The villagers waited for him at the gate. A shower of stones whistled about his ears, and the villagers shouted, "Sorcerer! Wolf's brat! Jungle demon! Go away! Buldeo, shoot!"

Buldeo's musket went off with a bang. The bullet missed Mowgli.

"More sorcery!" shouted the villagers. "He can turn bullets away. Buldeo, that shot hit your buffalo!"

Mowgli had not expected this kind of reaction. Akela told him that the villagers were like the pack. "They are casting you out," the wolf said.

"Last time I was cast out was because I was a man. This time it is because I am a wolf. Let us go, Akela," Mowgli said sadly.

By the light of the moon shining over the plain, the villagers saw Mowgli and the two wolves making their way back to the jungle.

CHAPTER 5
Return to the Council Rock

The moon was just going down when Mowgli and the two wolves came to the Council Rock. They stopped at Mother Wolf's cave.

"I have been cast out of the man pack, Mother," Mowgli shouted, "but I have Shere Khan's hide with me to keep my word to my first pack."

"It is well done," Mother Wolf said.

"Yes, it is well done." Bagheera's deep voice rose out of the thicket. He ran to Mowgli, and together they clambered up the Council Rock. The boy spread the skin out on the flat stone where Akela used to sit and pegged it down with four slivers of bamboo. Akela lay down upon it.

"Look well," Akela called, exactly as he had called when Mowgli was first brought there.

The pack had had no leader since Akela was overthrown. Out of habit, they returned his call. Some of them were lame from the traps they had fallen into. Some limped from bullet wounds. But they came out and saw Shere Khan's hide and the huge claws dangling at the end of the empty dangling feet.

"Have I kept my word?" Mowgli asked.

The wolves bayed, "Yes." One tattered wolf howled, "Lead us again, Akela. Lead us again, man-cub. We are tired of this lawlessness. We want to be the Free People again."

"No," Bagheera purred. "You fought for this. It is yours."

"Both the man pack and the wolf pack have cast me out," Mowgli said. "Now I will hunt alone in the jungle."

"And we will hunt with you," his brother cubs said.

Rikki-Tikki-Tavi

CHAPTER 1
A Remarkable Mongoose

Like all mongooses, Rikki-tikki-tavi was curious and friendly, and nothing frightened him. And like all mongooses, Rikki-tikki knew that he was the snake's archenemy. But Rikki-tikki was a young mongoose, and the snakes he met at the big bungalow in Segowlee cantonment were particularly wicked.

Rikki-tikki was like a little cat in his fur and his tail, but like a weasel in his head and his habits. His eyes and the end of his nose were pink. He could scratch himself wherever he pleased with any leg, front or back. And when he went looking for snakes, his tail bristled menacingly as he gave his piercing war cry, "Rikk-tikk-tikki-tikki-tchk!"

Rikki-tikki lived in a burrow until a summer flood washed him out of his home and down a roadside ditch. He took hold of a wisp of grass that was floating in the ditch and the next thing he knew, he was lying under the hot sun in the middle of a garden path.

"Here's a dead mongoose," a small boy said. "Let's have a funeral."

"Perhaps he isn't really dead," the boy's mother replied. "Let's take him in and dry him off."

So they took Rikki-tikki into their bungalow. The boy's father confirmed that the mongoose was not dead, so they wrapped Rikki-tikki in something warm and put him near the fire. Soon he opened his eyes and sneezed. Then he ran around the table, sat up, and put his fur in order, scratched himself, and jumped onto the boy's shoulder.

"Don't be frightened, Teddy," his father said. "The mongoose is making friends with you."

"He's tickling my chin," Teddy said.

"What a mischievous creature,"

Teddy's mother said. "But he seems quite tame."

"All mongooses are like that," her husband said. "If Teddy doesn't pick him up by the tail or try to put him in a cage, he'll happily run in and out of the house all day."

Rikki-tikki liked the raw meat that they gave him to eat, and he liked the family. To Rikki-tikki, the bungalow seemed full of interesting things and corners to explore.

That night Rikki-tikki ran into the nursery and climbed into bed with the boy. When Teddy's mother and father came to check on their son, Rikki-tikki was wide awake on the pillow.

"I don't like that," Teddy's mother said. "He may bite the child."

"He will do no such thing," Teddy's father said. "Teddy's safer with that little mongoose than if he had a bloodhound to watch him."

Early in the morning, Rikki-tikki came to breakfast on the veranda, riding on Teddy's shoulder. He sat on each family member's lap, one after the other, and they gave him bits of banana and boiled egg.

After breakfast, Rikki-tikki went to explore the garden. It was a large, half-cultivated area with big rosebushes, lime and orange trees, clumps of bamboos, and thickets of high grass. Rikki-tikki was delighted. "This is a splendid place to hunt," he said to himself.

CHAPTER 2
Who Is Nag?

While Rikki-tikki was poking around in the garden, he heard voices coming from a thorn bush. It was Darzee, the Tailorbird, and his wife. They had made a beautiful nest, which swayed under them as they sat on the rim and cried.

"What is the matter?" Rikki-tikki asked.

"One of our babies fell out of the nest yesterday and Nag ate him," Darzee said sadly.

"That is very sad," Rikki-tikki agreed. "But I am a stranger here. Who is Nag?"

Darzee and his wife cowered down in the nest without answering. A low hiss

rose up from the thick grass at the foot of the thorn bush, causing Rikki-tikki to jump back. Then Nag the big black cobra appeared, five feet long from tongue to tail. When he had lifted one-third of his body clear off the ground, he looked at Rikki-tikki with his cool, piercing eyes.

"I am Nag," the snake said. "Be afraid!"

Rikki-tikki was afraid, but not for long. Although he had never met a live cobra before, his mother had fed him dead ones, and he knew that a grown mongoose's business is to fight and eat snakes. Nag knew that, too, and was actually frightened of Rikki-tikki.

"Well," Rikki-tikki said, his tail bristling, "do you think it is right to eat fledglings out of a nest?"

"You eat eggs," Nag said. "Why shouldn't I eat birds?"

"Look behind you!" Darzee sang out.

Rikki-tikki jumped up in the air as

high as he could, just as the head of Nag's wicked wife, Nagaina, whizzed under him. He landed almost across her back. Rikki-tikki was afraid of the terrible lashing return stroke of the cobra. He bit—but not long enough—then he jumped clear of Nagaina's sweeping tail.

"Wicked Darzee!" Nag said.

Rikki-tikki's eyes grew red and hot—the sign that a mongoose is angry—and looked around him for the snakes. They were gone, and Rikki-tikki did not care

to follow them. It was no small thing for a young mongoose to escape a blow from behind, but he wasn't sure that he could manage two snakes at once. So he trotted off to the gravel path near the bungalow and sat down to think.

Teddy came running down the path and stooped to pet Rikki-tikki. Something wriggled in the dust. It was Karait, the brown snake. His bite was as deadly as the cobra's, but he was so small that people overlooked him.

Rikki-tikki's eyes grew red again, and he danced up to Karait. He didn't know that what he was doing was much more dangerous than fighting Nag. Karait struck out, and Rikki-tikki jumped sideways and tried to run in. But the wicked little head struck again, this time within a fraction of Rikki-tikki's shoulder. The little mongoose had to jump over the body, and Karait's head followed close on his heels.

Teddy had alerted his parents, who came running. His father had a stick ready, but by that time Karait was dead. Rikki-tikki was just about to eat Karait when he remembered that a full meal makes a slow mongoose.

Teddy's mother picked Rikki-tikki up from the dust and hugged him. "You've saved Teddy!" she cried.

CHAPTER 3

An Evil Plot

At dinner that evening, Rikki-tikki hopped playfully around the table. After all the fighting, he might have eaten three times his fill but he remembered that Nag and Nagaina waited somewhere in the garden.

After dinner, Teddy carried his new pet off to bed. But as soon as Teddy was asleep, Rikki-tikki went off for his nightly walk around the house. In the dark he met Chuchundra, the muskrat, who was creeping around the walls.

"Don't kill me," Chuchundra said, almost weeping. The muskrat was known for his timidity and never traveled far away from the walls.

"Do you think a snake killer kills muskrats?" Rikki-tikki asked scornfully.

"Those who kill snakes get killed by snakes," said Chuchundra. "How can I be sure that Nag won't mistake me for you some dark night?"

"There's no danger," Rikki-tikki said. "Nag is in the garden, and I know you don't go there."

"My cousin Chua, the rat, told me—" Chuchundra said, and then stopped.

"Told you what?" Rikki-tikki asked.

"Please hush! Nag is everywhere," Chuchundra warned.

"You must tell me right now. Quick, Chuchundra, or I'll bite you!" Rikki-tikki threatened.

Chuchundra sat down and cried until the tears rolled off his whiskers. "I am a poor muskrat," he sobbed. "I never had enough courage to run out into the middle of the room. I mustn't tell you anything. Can't you hear for yourself, Rikki-tikki?"

The house was perfectly still, but Rikki-tikki heard the dry scratch of snakes' scales on brickwork.

"That's two cobras crawling into the bathroom," Rikki-tikki said to himself.

Rikki-tikki ran off. His first stop was Teddy's bathroom, but no cobras were there. So Rikki-Tikki moved on to Teddy's mother's bathroom. At the bottom of the wall was a brick pulled out to make a sluice, or passage, for the bathwater. As Rikki-tikki crept closer, he heard the cobras whispering together outside in the moonlight.

"When there are no more people in the house, he will have to go away. Then the garden will be ours again," Nagaina hissed. "Go in quietly. The big man who killed Karait is the first one to bite. Then come out and get me and we will hunt for the mongoose together."

"I will go," Nag said uncertainly.

Rikki-tikki tingled all over in rage. Then Nag's head came through the sluice, and the five feet of his cold body followed it. Angry as he was, Rikki-tikki was very frightened when he saw the size of the cobra. Nag coiled himself up, raised his head, and looked into the dark bathroom. Rikki-tikki could see his eyes glittering.

"If I kill him here, Nagaina will know. If I fight him on the open floor, the odds are in his favor. What am I to do?" Rikki-tikki asked himself.

Nag moved back toward the opening

and spoke. "When Karait was killed, the man had a stick. When he comes in to bathe in the morning, he will not have a stick. I will wait here until he comes. Nagaina, do you hear me?"

No one answered, so Rikki-tikki knew Nagaina had gone away. Nag coiled himself around the bulge at the bottom of a water jar. After an hour, Rikki-tikki began to move slowly toward the jar. Nag was asleep.

"If I don't break his back on the first jump, he can still fight," Rikki-tikki

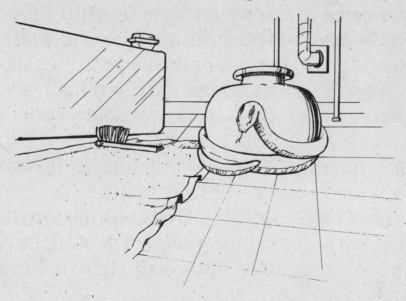

reasoned. He looked at the thickness of the neck below Nag's hood, but that was too much for him. And a bite near the tail would only make Nag savage.

"It must be the head," he decided. "The head above the hood, and I must not let go."

Then he jumped. Rikki-tikki braced his back against the bulge of the jar to hold down the head. This gave him a second to prepare for the onslaught. He was battered to and fro on the floor, up and down and around in great circles. His red eyes glowed, as he held on tight. Nag's body swooshed all over the floor, upsetting a soap dish and a bath brush.

Poor Rikki-tikki was dizzy and aching, certain that he would be shattered to pieces. Then he heard a thunderclap behind him. A hot wind knocked him over and red fire singed his fur. Teddy's father, wakened by the commotion in the bathroom, had just fired both barrels of a shotgun into Nag right behind the hood.

"It's the mongoose again, Alice. He has saved our lives!" the man said as Teddy's mother came running in.

Rikki-tikki dragged himself to Teddy's bedroom. He spent much of the rest of the night shaking himself to find out whether he was broken into forty pieces, as he imagined.

In the morning he was ready to deal with Nagaina. "She will be worse than five Nags, and there's no knowing when

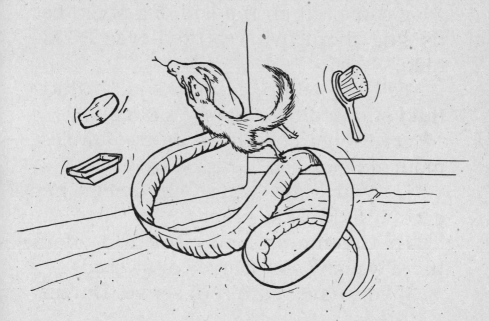

her eggs will hatch. I must go and see Darzee," he said.

Rikki-tikki ran to the thorn bush. Darzee was singing a song of triumph at the top of his voice. The news of Nag's death was all over the garden, for the sweeper had thrown the body on the garbage heap.

"Oh, you stupid tuft of feathers!" Rikki-tikki said angrily. "Where's Nagaina?"

"Nagaina came to the bathroom sluice and called for Nag," Darzee reported. "Nag came out on the end of a stick. Let us sing about the great, red-eyed Rikki-tikki!"

"Tell me where Nagaina is," Rikki-tikki shouted over Darzee's singing.

"On the garbage heap by the stables, mourning for Nag," Darzee said.

"Do you know where she keeps her eggs?" Rikki-tikki asked.

"In the melon bed. She hid them there weeks ago," Darzee answered.

"If you have a grain of sense, Darzee,

you will fly off to the stables and pretend that your wing is broken," Rikki-tikki said. "Let Nagaina chase you away to this bush so I can get to the melon bed without her knowing."

Just because he knew that Nagaina's children were born in eggs, like his own, Darzee didn't think it was fair to kill them. But his wife knew that cobra's eggs meant young cobras later on. So she flew off from the nest and left Darzee to keep the babies warm.

She fluttered in front of Nagaina by the garbage heap and cried out, "The boy in the house threw a stone at me and broke my wing." Then she fluttered more desperately than ever.

Nagaina lifted up her head and hissed, "You warned Rikki-tikki when I would have killed him." Then she moved toward the bird, sliding over the dust. "My husband now lies on the garbage heap, but before night comes that boy will lie very still. What is the use of running away? I am sure to catch you."

When Rikki-tikki heard them going up the path from the stables, he raced toward the melon bed. Hidden in the warm litter above the melons, he found twenty-five eggs about the size of a bantam's eggs, but with whitish skin instead of shell. They were just about to hatch.

He bit off the tops of the eggs and crushed the young cobras. When there were only three eggs left, Rikki-tikki heard Darzee's wife screaming, "Rikki-tikki, I led Nagaina toward the house. She has gone onto the veranda!"

Rikki-tikki smashed two eggs and took off with the third egg in his mouth.

CHAPTER 4
Nagaina's Revenge

Teddy and his parents sat at the breakfast table, but they weren't eating. They sat as still as stones. Nagaina was coiled up on the matting by Teddy's chair, within easy striking distance of the boy's bare leg.

Teddy's eyes were fixed on his father, who whispered, "Sit still, Teddy. You mustn't move."

Then Rikki-tikki came up and cried, "Turn and fight, Nagaina!"

"All in good time," she hissed, without moving her eyes. "I will settle my account with you presently. Look at your friends, Rikki-tikki. They are afraid. If you come a step nearer, I will strike."

"Look at your eggs," Rikki-tikki countered, "in the melon bed near the wall. Go and look, Nagaina!"

Nagaina shifted her gaze and saw the egg on the veranda. "Give it to me," she said.

"What price for a snake's egg? For a young cobra? For a young king cobra? For the very last of the brood? The ants are eating all the others down by the melon bed," Rikki-tikki said.

Nagaina spun around. Rikki-tikki saw Teddy's father catch Teddy by the shoulder and drag him across the table, safe and out of Nagaina's reach.

"Tricked!" Rikki-tikki chuckled. "The boy is safe." He jumped up and down as he told Nagaina how he had killed Nag. "He was dead before the man blew him in two. Now come and fight with me."

"Give me the egg and I will go away and never come back," she said.

"You will go to the garbage heap with Nag. The big man has gone for his gun!

Fight!" Rikki-tikki yelled.

Nagaina charged out at him. Rikki-tikki jumped up and backward. Again and again and again she struck, and each time her head came down with a whack on the matting. Rikki-tikki danced in a circle to get behind her, and Nagaina turned to keep her head to his head.

Rikki-tikki had forgotten the egg, which still lay on the veranda. Nagaina came nearer and nearer to it until at last she caught it in her mouth. She turned to the veranda steps and flew

off down the path, heading straight for the long grass by the thorn bush.

Rikki-tikki followed her. Darzee was still singing, but his wife flew off her nest and flapped her wings about the snake's head. If Darzee had helped, they might have turned her, but Nagaina only lowered her hood and went on. Still, in the instant's delay, Rikki-tikki caught up to her. When she plunged into the rat-hole where she and Nag lived, his little white teeth were clenched onto her tail.

Following a cobra into a hole is not something that many mongooses would do. Rikki-tikki knew that he might never come out, but he held on and stuck out his feet to act as brakes on the dark slope of the hot, moist earth.

When the grass by the mouth of the hole stopped waving, Darzee said, "It is all over with Rikki-tikki! We must sing his death song."

While Darzee sang, the grass quivered again, and up popped Rikki-tikki!

He shook some of the dust out of his fur and sneezed. "Yes, it is all over," he said. After all of his hard work, Rikki-tikki certainly deserved the long nap he took right there in the grass.

Later, when he got to the bungalow, Teddy and his parents petted and hugged him. That night he ate all he could eat and went to bed on Teddy's shoulder, which is where Teddy's mother saw him when she came in to check on them.

"He saved our lives," she said to her

husband in amazement.

Rikki-tikki had a right to be proud, but he did not grow too proud. He cheerfully kept the garden as a mongoose should keep it, with tooth and jump and spring and bite, until no cobra dared to show its head within the walls.

Toomai of the Elephants

CHAPTER 1
The Good Servant

Kala Nag was a huge elephant that had served the Indian government for forty-seven years. Kala Nag means Black Snake. Before his little milk tusks had fallen out, his mother told him that elephants that were always afraid to get hurt. Kala Nag took her advice and became the bravest and best-loved elephant in the government's service.

Now he was nearly seventy years old, and had many memories from his years of service. His many adventures included carrying tents weighing hundreds of pounds on the march in Upper India; being hoisted into a ship at the end of a steam crane and traveling for days across the water; and being sent thousands of miles south to haul and pile big balks of teak in the timber yards at Moulmein.

After that he was taken off timber hauling and put to work catching wild elephants in the Garo hills. The Indian government strictly preserved the country's elephants. There was one whole department that did nothing but hunt them, catch them, and break them in. Then the elephants were sent all over the

country, as they were needed for work.

Kala Nag towered more than ten feet above the ground, and his tusks had been cut off short at five feet. They were bound around the ends with copper bands to prevent them from splitting. He could do more with those stumps than any untrained elephant could do with the real sharpened ones.

The men called on Kala Nag when the wild elephants needed taming. After many weeks being driven across the hills, the wild creatures were taken into the last stockade. The big drop gate, made of tree trunks lashed together, jarred down behind them.

Then Kala Nag, at the men's command, would charge into the uproar to pick out the biggest, wildest tusker and hammer it into submission while the men on the backs of the other elephants roped and tied the smaller ones.

Brave Kala Nag was feared because he knew everything there was to know about fighting. He had even stood up more than once to the charge of a wounded tiger.

"There is nothing that the Black Snake fears except me!" said Big Toomai, his driver. Big Toomai was the son of Black Toomai and the grandson of Toomai of the Elephants. They all had driven Kala Nag. "He has seen three generations of us feed and groom him, and he will live to see four," Big Toomai predicted.

"Kala Nag is afraid of me, too," Little Toomai said, standing up to his full height—four feet. Little Toomai was ten years old and was Big Toomai's eldest son. According to custom, when he grew up he would be the one to ride on Kala Nag's neck and handle the heavy iron ankus, the elephant goad, that had been worn smooth by his father, his grandfather, and his great-grandfather.

Little Toomai had played with the end of Kala Nag's trunk before he could walk. He had taken the elephant down to the water as soon as the boy could

walk. Kala Nag remembered how Big Toomai had held the little brown baby under Kala Nag's tusks and had told the elephant to salute his future master. So Kala Nag loved the boy and would not disobey his shrill little orders, although he knew that the boy was wild.

Little Toomai liked to scramble up bridle paths that only an elephant could take. He came to love the dip into the valley below, the glimpses of the wild elephants browsing miles away.

The hunters knew that Little Toomai was as useful as three boys. He would wave his torch and yell with the best of them. But when the driving began, Little Toomai showed his real worth. The Keddah—or stockade—became a scene of frenzy. Little Toomai would climb onto one of the stockade posts, and as soon as there was a lull, he would cry, "Go on, Black Snake! Give him the tusk! Hit him!" Kala Nag would fight the wild beasts until they could no longer fight back. The old elephant catchers would wipe the sweat out of their eyes and nod to Little Toomai, who was wriggling with joy on the top of his post.

One night, Little Toomai slid down from his post and slipped in between the elephants. He threw up the loose end of a rope, which had dropped, to a driver who was trying to get a hold of the leg of a young calf that was kicking up a storm. Kala Nag saw the boy, caught him in his trunk, and handed him up to Big Toomai, who slapped him hard and put him back onto the post.

The next morning, Little Toomai got a scolding from his father. He was worried that Petersen Sahib, the head of all the stockade operations—the man who caught all of the elephants for the Indian government—would hear about it. Petersen Sahib knew more about the ways of elephants than any man alive.

"So you think you are big enough to go elephant catching on your own?" his father asked. "Now those foolish hunters have told Peterson Sahib about it." Big Toomai had a higher rank and pay than the hunters, and he did not want his son to be a hunter and live the harsh camp life.

"What will happen?" Little Toomai asked.

"Petersen Sahib may require you to be an elephant catcher, to sleep anywhere in these fever-filled jungles, and at last to be trampled to death in the stockade. It is good that this nonsense has ended safely. Next week the catching is over, and we of the plains will be sent back to our stations. Remember, my son, Kala Nag will obey no one but me, so I must go with him into the stockade. But he is only a fighting elephant, and he does not help rope them."

Little Toomai could see that his father was very angry, but he really wanted to be a hunter.

"Go and wash Kala Nag and attend to his ears. See that there are no thorns in his feet, or Petersen Sahib will surely make you a wild hunter. Go!" his father ordered.

Little Toomai went off without saying a word. He told Kala Nag all about it while he was examining the elephant's feet. "No matter," Little Toomai said as he turned up the fringe of one of Kala Nag's huge ears. "Now Petersen Sahib knows my name. Who knows what will come of it?"

CHAPTER 2
The Man
Who Knew Elephants

The men of the camps spent the next few days getting the elephants together. Petersen Sahib came in on his she-elephant, Pudmini. He had been paying the hunters at the other camps since the season was coming to an end. As the men were paid, they went back to their elephants and joined the line that stood ready to depart. The regular men of the stockade—the catchers and hunters and beaters—who stayed in the jungle throughout the year sat on the backs of elephants belonging to Petersen Sahib's permanent force.

Big Toomai went up to the clerk, who sat at a table under a tree, with Little

Toomai behind him. Machua Appa, the head tracker, said in an undertone to another man, "There goes a boy who has a way with the elephants. It's a pity to send that boy back to the plains."

Now Petersen Sahib had ears all over him, as a man must have who listens to the most silent of all living things— the wild elephant. He turned in his seat on Pudmini's back and asked, "Who is this man?"

"Not a man, but a boy," Machua

Appa replied, pointing at Little Toomai. "He went into the stockade during the last drive and threw Barmao the rope when we were trying to get that young calf away from his mother."

"He can throw a rope? He is smaller than a picket-pin. What is your name, little one?" Petersen Sahib asked.

Little Toomai was too frightened to speak. Kala Nag was behind him, and when Little Toomai made a sign with his hand, the elephant caught the boy up in his trunk and held him level with Pudmini's forehead—right in front of Petersen Sahib! Little Toomai covered his face with his hands, for he was only a child, and except where elephants were concerned, he was just as bashful as a child could be.

"Good trick," Petersen Sahib said, applauding. "Did you teach that to the elephant to help you steal green corn from the roofs of the houses when the ears are put out to dry?"

"Not green corn, the Protector of the

Poor," Little Toomai said. "Melons." All of the men sitting around roared with laughter. Most of them had taught their elephants that trick when they were boys. Little Toomai was hanging eight feet up in the air but wished that he were eight feet underground.

"He is Toomai, my son, Sahib," Big Toomai said, scowling. "He is a wild boy."

Petersen Sahib shook his head. "A boy who can face a full stockade at his age is quite skilled," he said. Turning to the boy, he added, "Here are four coins, little one. You have a head under that great mop of hair. In time, you may become a hunter. But remember, the stockades are not good for children to play in."

Little Toomai gasped. "Must I never go there, Sahib?" he asked.

"You can go to the stockades when you have seen the elephants dance. Come to me after you've seen it and I will let you go into all of the stockades," Petersen Sahib said.

The men laughed again. When the elephant catchers say, "When the elephants dance," that means never. There are great clearings hidden away in the forests that are called elephants' ballrooms. They are only found by accident, and no man has ever seen the elephants dance.

Kala Nag put Little Toomai down. The boy bowed again to Petersen Sahib, and then went away with his father. He gave the coins as a gift to his mother, who was nursing his baby brother. Together they rode on Kala Nag's back to go with the line of elephants down the hill path and back to the plains.

"What did Petersen Sahib mean by the elephant dance?" Little Toomai whispered to his mother.

His father heard him and said, "That you would never be one of these hill-buffaloes," meaning the trackers who were beneath his position.

The elephants were particularly difficult during the ride. One of the

drivers said, "These new elephants are possessed, or else they can smell their companions in the jungle." Kala Nag went to work, quieting the unruly beasts.

Another driver said, "They know that the drives have ended for the season. So tonight, all of the wild elephants will—"

"What will they do?" Little Toomai called out.

"They will dance. If your father is wise, he will double-chain his pickets tonight," the driver answered.

"For forty years, father and son, we have tended elephants, and we have never heard such moonshine about dancing elephants," Big Toomai said.

The men argued back and forth about the dancing elephants, splashing through the rivers as they traveled to a receiving camp for the new beasts.

CHAPTER 3
A Wild Adventure

When they arrived at the camp, the men chained the elephants by their hind legs to big stumps of pickets. Extra ropes were fitted to the new elephants, and the fodder was piled before them. Then the hill drivers went back to Petersen Sahib through the afternoon light, telling the plains drivers to be extra careful that night and laughing when the plains drivers asked the reason.

Little Toomai gave Kala Nag his supper. Afterward, the boy wandered through the camp in search of a tom-tom to play. He was very happy that Petersen Sahib had noticed him. A vendor selling sweets in the camp lent him a little tom-tom, and Little Toomai happily sat down cross-legged in front of Kala Nag to play.

He could hear his mother in the camp hut singing his little brother to sleep. He punctuated each verse with his drum until he felt drowsy himself and stretched out near Kala Nag to sleep.

Finally the elephants began to settle down. As was their custom, they lay down one after the other until only Kala Nag was left standing at the far right of the line. Through the usual night noises of trees and creatures rustling about, the elephant listened closely to some far-off sound.

Little Toomai slept for some time. When he awoke, the moonlight shone brilliantly, and Kala Nag was standing up with his ears pitched. Little Toomai watched the elephant and strained to hear a noise that seemed ever so far away—the *hoot-toot* of a wild elephant.

The other elephants heard it and

began straining against their chains. The beasts' grunting woke the men. They came out and drove in the picket pegs with big mallets and tightened the ropes. Big Toomai took off Kala Nag's leg chain in order to shackle another elephant that needed a stronger hold. He slipped a loop of grass string around Kala Nag's leg and told the elephant to stay put. Like his father and grandfather before him, Big Toomai had done this hundreds of times before. Kala Nag did not answer to the order by gurgling, as he usually did. He stood still, looking out across the moonlight up to the Garo hills, his head a little raised and his ears spread like fans.

Before retiring to the hut, Big Toomai told his son to tend Kala Nag if the beast grew restless in the night. Little Toomai was just falling off to sleep again when he heard the grass string snap. Seeing Kala Nag start to move, Little Toomai got up to follow, barefoot and covered in one small rag.

"Take me with you, Kala Nag!" the boy called. The elephant turned and took three strides back to the boy. He put down his trunk, swung Little Toomai up to his neck, and then slipped into the dark forest. The big elephant moved silently, drifting through the thick Garo forest as though it were smoke. Little Toomai knew that they traveled uphill, but even though he watched the stars through the trees, he could not tell in which direction.

When Kala Nag had reached the crest of the hill, Little Toomai leaned forward to get a better look at his sur- roundings. A big, brown fruit-eating bat brushed past his ear. A porcupine's quills rattled in the thicket. And in the darkness between the tree stems, he heard a wild boar digging hard in the moist warm earth.

Kala Nag began to move, no longer silently, and the branches closed over Little Toomai's head. Soon the elephant was proceeding in a mad rush, with Little Toomai clinging tightly to the elephant's neck. The undergrowth on both sides of them ripped with a noise like torn canvas, and the saplings that Kala Nag heaved away right and left with his shoulders sprang back again and banged him on the flank. Long trails of creepers, all matted together, hung from his tusks as he swung his head from side to side.

Soon they came to a marshy area. Kala Nag's feet sunk down into the wet earth. The night mist at the bottom of the valley chilled Little Toomai. The boy heard splashing and the rush of running water. Kala Nag strode through the bed of a river, feeling his way at each step. Above the noise of the water, Little Toomai heard more splashing and also some trumpeting both upstream and down.

Through his chattering teeth, Little Toomai exclaimed, "The elephants are out dancing tonight!"

Kala Nag rose out of the water, blew his trunk, and began another climb. Kala Nag no longer had to clear his own path, because the elephants before him had made one six feet wide. A large band of elephants must have gone that way only a few minutes before. Little Toomai looked back and saw behind him a great wild tusker with his eyes glowing like hot coals. The creature was lifting himself out of the misty river. Then the trees closed up again, and they went on and up. The sound of trumpeting and breaking branches rang out on every side.

At last Kala Nag stood still between two tree trunks at the top of the hill. The trees were part of a circle that grew around a large open space. The ground had been trampled as hard as a brick floor. Some trees grew in the center of the clearing, but their bark was rubbed away, and the white wood beneath shone out in the moonlight. Creepers and flowers hung down from the branches, but within the clearing there was nothing but trampled earth.

CHAPTER 4

The Dance
of the Elephants

The elephants began to move out of the shadows and into the clearing. There were ancient beasts, white-tusked males, slow-footed she-elephants with their calves, and young elephants with their tusks just beginning to show. Little Toomai could hear more elephants crashing through the undergrowth outside of the clearing.

When there was no sound of any more elephants arriving, Kala Nag came out from between the trees and went into the middle of the crowd. The rest of the elephants began to sway and talk in their own language. After a while an elephant trumpeted, signaling for the

others to follow suit. The noise was beyond deafening and caused showers of dew to fall from the trees. Then the trumpeting was replaced by dull thumping that rose to a rumble and became a thunderous roar.

The elephants were stamping all together now. The ground rocked and shivered. The dancing lasted two hours or more.

The booming stopped with the first rays of sun. Little Toomai had not gotten the ringing out of his head before the elephants had disappeared without a trace. Only Kala Nag, Pudmini, and one other elephant that had escaped from a camp were left.

As tired as he was, Little Toomai just sat and stared at the clearing. Now he understood what the tramping was all about. The elephants had created their own ballroom! "Kala Nag, my lord, let us keep by Pudmini and go to Petersen Sahib's camp," he said.

Two hours later they entered Petersen Sahib's camp just as he was eating his breakfast. The elephants were in utter disarray, and Little Toomai's face was gray and pinched. "I have seen the elephants dance in their ballroom!" he announced joyously. Then he slid off Kala Nag's neck in a dead faint.

A while later, he was lying very contentedly in Petersen Sahib's hammock. The seasoned hunters sat around him. They looked at him as if he were a ghost as he told his tale.

Soon everyone in the camp gathered by the blazing campfires for a feast, and Little Toomai was the hero of it all!

Machua Appa leaped to his feet and held Little Toomai high in the air above his head. "This little one shall now be called Toomai of the Elephants. He shall become a great tracker, and he will come to no harm in his travels."

The elephants flung up their trunks and saluted. And it was all for the sake of Little Toomai, who had seen what no man has ever seen: the wild night dance of the elephants in the heart of the Garo hills.

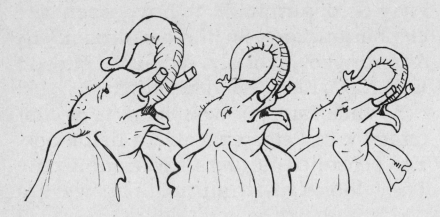

About the Author

Rudyard Kipling was born in Bombay, India, in 1865. His parents were both artistic and literary. For unknown reasons, Kipling was left at the age of six with a foster family in England. He lived there for five years. In later years, he wrote about his hardships in a short story, "Baa Baa Black Sheep" (1888) and in a novel, *The Light That Failed* (1890).

After his college graduation in 1882, Kipling started work as a journalist in India. He published *Plain Tales from the Hills* in 1888, which became an instant success.

Kipling married an American author, Caroline Balestier, in 1892. They moved to Vermont for four years, where Kipling wrote his most famous novel, *The Jungle Book* (1894).

In 1907, Kipling was awarded the Nobel Prize for Literature, making him the first English writer to receive this honor. Throughout his career, Kipling wrote hundreds of short stories, poems, and novels for children and adults. He died in London in 1936.

Adventures of Huckleberry Finn
The Adventures of Pinocchio
The Adventures of Robin Hood
The Adventures of Sherlock Holmes
The Adventures of Tom Sawyer
Alice in Wonderland
Anne of Green Gables
Beauty and the Beast
Black Beauty
The Call of the Wild
Frankenstein
Great Expectations
Gulliver's Travels
Heidi
Jane Eyre
Journey to the Center of the Earth
The Jungle Book
King Arthur and the Knights of the Round Table
The Legend of Sleepy Hollow & Rip Van Winkle
A Little Princess
Little Women
Moby Dick
Oliver Twist
Peter Pan
The Prince and the Pauper
Pygmalion
Rebecca of Sunnybrook Farm
Robinson Crusoe
The Secret Garden
Swiss Family Robinson
The Time Machine
Treasure Island
20,000 Leagues Under the Sea
White Fang
The Wind in the Willows
The Wizard of Oz